The Runaway CHICKEN

BY KIKI THORPE

ILLUSTRATED BY MAINE DIAZ

Kane Press
New York

For Knox and Wade, who always let
us find the eggs—K.T.

To the ones who let their feelings
guide the way.—M.D.

Library of Congress Cataloging-in-Publication Data
Names: Thorpe, Kiki, author. | Diaz, Maine, illustrator.
Title: The runaway chicken / by Kiki Thorpe ; illustrated by Maine Diaz.
Description: New York : Kane Press, 2018. | Series: Makers make it work |
Summary: Maddy finds a chicken crossing a city street and, after trying to find her owner,
comes up with a way to build her a coop.
Identifiers: LCCN 2017020313 (print) | LCCN 2017036877 (ebook) | ISBN
9781575659923 (ebook) | ISBN 9781575659916 (pbk) | ISBN 9781635920123 (reinforced
library binding)
Subjects: | CYAC: Chickens—Fiction. | Building—Fiction. | Lost and found possessions—
Fiction. | City and town life—Fiction.
Classification: LCC PZ7.T3974 (ebook) | LCC PZ7.T3974 Rw 2018 (print) | DDC
[E]—dc23
LC record available at https://lccn.loc.gov/2017020313

33614082273722

10 9 8 7 6 5 4 3 2 1

First published in the United States of America in 2018 by Kane Press, Inc.
Printed in China

Makers Make It Work is a trademark of Kane Press, Inc.

Book Design: Michelle Martinez

Visit us online at **www.kanepress.com**

Like us on Facebook
facebook.com/kanepress

Follow us on Twitter
@KanePress

My best friend and I were walking home from school. "Hey, Dave," I said. "Why is a chicken crossing the road?"

Dave rolled his eyes. "That's an old joke, Maddy."

"I'm not joking," I told him. "Look!"

A real chicken was crossing the street in front of my house!

We live in the city. There are plenty of cars, buses, pigeons, and people. But I'd never seen a chicken before. That bird needed help—fast.

I chased the chicken down the sidewalk. Let me tell you, catching a chicken isn't easy. But I finally grabbed it.

"What are you planning to do with a chicken?" Dave asked. He doesn't like animals as much as I do.

"It must be lost," I said. "I'm going to find its owner."

I took the chicken home. My mom freaked out. My dad freaked out. But they calmed down when I explained my plan.

"I'll put up signs," I said. "That way its owner will know where to find it."

"It must have gotten loose from someone's coop," Dad said.

A *coop* is a building where chickens are kept.

That afternoon, Dave and I made signs. We hung them all over the neighborhood.

I was sure someone would call. But no one did.

I guess the chicken was going to live with us for a while. It needed a name.

"How about 'Dinner'?" Dad suggested.

"Very funny," I said. "I was thinking 'Henrietta.'"

Mom looked worried. "The chicken isn't a pet, Maddy. It will have to go back to its real owner," she told me.

"I know," I said. "I just want her to feel at home."

We watched Henrietta steal our cat Petey's food. "She looks pretty at home to me," Dad said.

That night I put Henrietta in the laundry room. When I woke up— Wow, what a mess! My parents made me clean it up.

"Maybe we should take Henrietta to the local animal shelter," Mom said. "They'll know how to care for her. Her owner may look for her there, too."

Mom had a point. Chickens do not make good house pets!

Poultry is another name for chickens and other birds, like ducks and turkeys.

Mom helped me load Henrietta into Petey's cat carrier.

But when we got to the animal shelter . . .

"We don't take poultry," the woman at the desk told us.

13

Henrietta came back home. Secretly, I was glad. But then things got worse. Henrietta ate the houseplants.

She scared Petey. And her squawking drove us all crazy.

BOK-BOK-BU-BOK!

One day, she laid an egg in my dad's sneaker.

CRUNCH!

He didn't find it until he put his shoes on.

My family had had enough. "That chicken has got to go," Dad said.

"Dad, no!" I cried. "I can't put Henrietta out on the street!"

"Then find a better place for her," Mom told me.

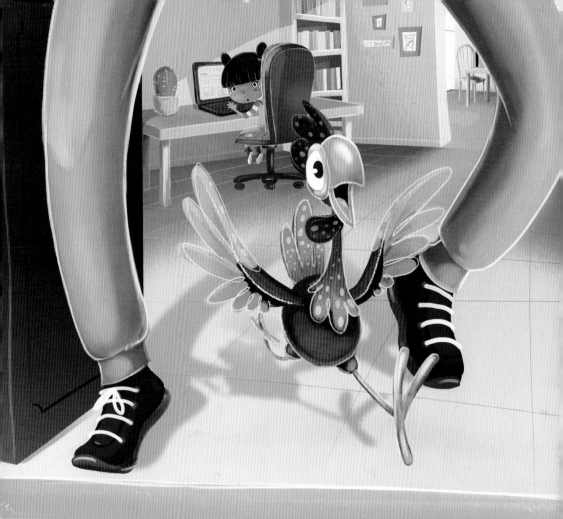

Where was I going to keep a chicken in the city? I couldn't just leave her in the yard. Dogs or cats could get her. I looked into buying a chicken coop. But they all cost over a hundred dollars. Yikes!

While I was deciding what to do, Henrietta escaped!

"Come back!" I yelled.

Luckily, Henrietta didn't get far. I spotted her on top of my neighbor's trashcan.

Suddenly I had a great idea. I could make that old doghouse into a coop for Henrietta!

"Are you throwing away this doghouse?" I asked my neighbor, Mr. Jackson.

"We don't need it," Mr. Jackson explained. "Rex is too old to sleep outside. He has a nice bed in the kitchen now."

I guess it's true. One person's trash is another person's treasure.

That afternoon, we moved the doghouse into our backyard.

Mom helped me clean it out. Then we got to work. We read that chickens like lots of air. Mom pulled off a couple boards with a crowbar to let more air flow through. We covered the gaps with wire to keep other animals out.

Woodworking is the craft of making things out of wood.

The doghouse needed a door to keep Henrietta safe and cozy. Dad helped me measure the space.

Measure twice, cut once. That means plan carefully before taking action.

Then we sawed a door from a piece of plywood. We used a screwdriver to add hinges and a latch.

We added a stick as roost for Henrietta to perch on.

Always wear goggles and make sure a grown-up is with you when you're woodworking. Safety comes first!

We built a nesting box where Henrietta could lay eggs. I did all the hammering!

Around the coop, we built a wooden frame with chicken wire. Henrietta would have a safe place to run around. Then we painted the henhouse. Even Dave helped.

Need a hammer?
A wrench? A screwdriver?
An organized toolbox will help
you find the right tool easily.

Finally the coop was ready.

"I can't believe you built that yourself!" Dave said.

"Nice work, Maddy," Mom added. Dad patted me on the back.

I picked up Henrietta. But before I could put her inside . . . she flew the coop!

Oh no! Not again!

We chased Henrietta down the street and around the corner.

"Stop that chicken!" I yelled to a man walking down the street.

He caught her!

"Is this your chicken?" the man asked. Henrietta sat calmly in his arms.

"Yes," I said.

"I lost one just like her last week," he said.

My heart sank. "I found her last week," I told him. "She must be yours."

I couldn't believe it. Now we'd found Henrietta's owner? After I had made a coop? After she was part of our family?

"My name is Joe," the man said. "Did you take care of her all week?"

"I did." I told him how I'd found Henrietta in the street. I told him how hard I'd tried to find her owner. I even told him about the chicken coop we'd built.

Joe listened carefully. Then, to my surprise, he asked to see the coop.

"Nice work!" he said when I showed him.

Joe told us he keeps chickens in his backyard. He even has a vegetable garden on his roof! "I'm an urban farmer," Joe explained.

"You know, Maddy," he went on. "You'd make a great urban farmer yourself. Maybe you should keep Henrietta."

I could keep her?

Hooray!

Our chicken coop has really worked out.
Mom and Dad like Henrietta so much now.
They're even thinking of getting more chickens!

And now I know why the chicken crossed the road—to find her way home!

Learn Like a Maker

Maddy saw something that was being thrown away and transformed it into something new and useful. With a little imagination, a well-stocked toolbox, and some help from her family, she was able to make just what she needed!

Look Back

- ⊗ Pages 20–22 describe how Maddy and her parents turned the old doghouse into a chicken coop. What tools did they use?

- ⊗ Look at pages 28–29. How is an urban farmer different than a traditional farmer? How are they similar?

Try This!

Build a Birdhouse

You will need a milk carton, glue, scissors, paints, a popsicle stick, a hole punch, and ribbon or string.

- ⊗ First, cut a quarter-sized hole, or larger, in the side of the milk carton.

- ⊗ Next, decorate the milk carton with non-toxic paints, so it's safe for the birds.

- ⊗ For a perch, glue a stick to the bottom of your birdhouse.

- ⊗ Then use string or ribbon to hang it outside.

Watch what kind of birds visit your birdhouse. Do you think different birds would visit a different type of birdhouse? How could you create one that would attract different birds?